SEVEN DELIGHTFUL STORIES
FOR EVERY DAY

Retold by Dov Peretz Elkins

Illustrated by Zely Smekhov

PITSPOPANY

NEW YORK ◆ JERUSALEM

ALSO AVAILABLE IN THIS SERIES:

Seven Animals Wag Their Tales
Seven Animal Stories For Children

Published by Pitspopany Press
Text Copyright © 2000 by Dov Peretz Elkins
Illustrations Copyright © 2000 by Zely Smekhov

Design: Tiffen Studios (T.C. Peterseil)

PITSPOPANY PRESS books may be purchased for educational or special sales by contacting:

Marketing Director, Pitspopany Press
40 East 78th Street, Suite 16D
New York, New York 10021
Fax: (212) 472-6253
E-mail: pop@netvision.net.il
Web: www.pitspopany.com

ISBN: 1-930143-02-8 Cloth
ISBN: 1-930143-03-6 Softcover

Printed in Hong Kong

CONTENTS

DEDICATED TO C.A.J.E.
The Coalition For The Advancement Of Jewish Education
and
To all its teachers who share themselves and
their experiences

ACKNOWLEDGMENTS

The author would like to thank the following early childhood experts for their assistance in reading and giving feedback on the stories in this book. Their help was invaluable in adjusting vocabulary, style and content to the appropriate age.

Lyndall Miller, Judi Felber, Melanie Berman, Marcia Posner, Sylvia Avner, Sandra Hoffman, Pam Swallow, Nancy Kraus, Maxine Sigal Handelman and Joan Levin.

Appreciation is also extended to my dear friend Peninnah Schram, master storyteller, who gave freely of her advice, time and expertise, and for permission to adapt her version of "Elijah's Three Wishes."

Yaacov Peterseil has been an insightful and gentle editor, without whose guidance and cooperation this book would not have been created.

Dov Peretz Elkins

SEVEN
DELIGHTFUL
STORIES
FOR
EVERY
DAY

Miriam's Mysterious Well Of Water

Why is it that sometimes you get what you pray for and sometimes you don't?

The Israelite people were slaves for many years to the cruel King Pharaoh in Egypt.

When they finally left the wicked land of Egypt, the Israelites walked across the dry desert called Sinai, toward the Promised Land of Israel. At first they were very happy that they were not slaves anymore. They sang happy songs.

But after they had walked for a long time, they couldn't sing any more. Their throats were very dry. They complained to Moses, their leader.

"We are thirsty," they cried out to Moses. "Why did you lead us out of Egypt? We are now in a terrible desert where there is no water to drink!"

Moses went to talk to his sister Miriam. He told her how worried he was that the people did not have any water to drink.

"What shall we do?" he asked her.

Miriam was a very kind person. She would always share what little food and water she had with others more hungry and thirsty than she.

"I will pray to God for water," said Miriam. "God will give us water to drink."

God wanted to reward Miriam because of her kindness to the people. So God listened to her prayers, and made a well of water in the desert. From this well, the people always had water to drink.

"Thank you so much," said the people to Miriam.

"We are so happy that we have water to drink."

After a while, the people walked to a new resting place in the desert. They were sorry to leave the well.

"Without Miriam's well of water, what shall we drink?" they asked Moses.

"Don't worry," Moses told the people. "God will give us more water."

But when they arrived at the new resting place in the desert, they couldn't find any water. They were very sad. What if Miriam prayed again to God and God did not send a well for them to drink from?

Suddenly, one of the women called out:

"Look," she said, "I see a well!"

The people looked. They could not believe their eyes.

"Another well!" they said.

As they walked closer to the well, they saw that it was the very same well from which they had drunk at their last resting place. The well had followed them from their old resting place to their new one.

"I know why we have our well of water again," Moses told the people. "It is because of the kindness of Miriam. She loves the people of Israel, and always helps us when we are hungry or thirsty. Because of her kindness, God has brought this well to our new resting place."

From that time on, the well was known as *Miriam's Well*.

And throughout all their wanderings in the desert, the Israelite people had a well of water with them, a magical well that was always filled with cool, pure water.

THINKING THOUGHTS

* Why do you think God listened to Miriam's prayers?
* What are some of the things you pray for?
* How do you think God decides whose prayers to answer?

What Can We Promise God?

Here's one reason the Jewish people will always survive

Forty days after the Israelite people left Egypt, they came to Mount Sinai. Moses climbed to the top of the mountain, and God spoke to him.

"I have a gift for you and your people, Moses," said God.

"What is the gift?" asked Moses, feeling honored and excited.

"This is a very important gift," answered God. "It is the most precious treasure in all the world.

"It is called the Torah."

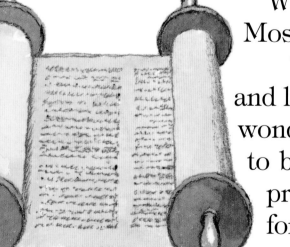

"What is the Torah?" asked Moses.

"The Torah contains stories and laws that show how to live a wonderful life. Therefore, I want to be certain that the Torah is properly guarded and cared for."

Moses came down the mountain and told the people of the great gift that God had promised them, the gift of the Torah.

"Will you promise to follow its rules, and study its stories?" asked Moses.

"Yes, we will!" answered the people.

Moses went back to God with the good news. "The people have promised that they will follow the rules and study the Torah."

God replied, "How can I be sure the people will keep their promise?"

Moses went back to the people again.

"God wants to know how we will be certain to keep our promise to obey the Torah."

One of the people called out to Moses. "The memory of Abraham and Sarah will help us keep our promise. They are the father and mother of the Israelites. That should please God greatly."

"An excellent idea," said Moses.

Moses climbed up the mountain and told God that the memory of Abraham and Sarah, the father and mother of the Israelite

people, would help the people keep their promise.

God replied: "Just because Abraham and Sarah listened to Me does not mean the Israelites will listen to Me. I need a better guarantee."

Moses went back to the people and told them that God wanted a better guarantee that the people would keep their promise to obey the Torah.

Another person in the crowd called out, "How about the great prophets of Israel? They will help us keep our promise."

All the people nodded their heads in agreement.

Moses climbed Mount Sinai and said to God: "I am happy to tell You that the people have another idea. The great prophets will help us keep our promise. Now can we have the precious gift of the Torah?"

"But the people will not always listen to the prophets," answered God. "Not even to a great prophet like you, Moses."

Once again Moses came down the mountain and spoke with the people

14

of Israel. "The prophets are not enough. God wants a better guarantee."

"I know!" shouted a child from the crowd. "I know! We, the children, will promise to keep the Torah."

"What a wonderful idea," said Moses, with great relief. "I think that is the best idea yet."

When Moses told God the children of the Israelites would guarantee to keep the Torah, God was very pleased.

"Here, Moses," God said. "Here is the Torah. Now I know for certain that the people will obey My Torah, forever."

THINKING THOUGHTS

* Why did God like the idea of the children promising to keep the Torah?
* What promises did you ever make to your family and friends?
* Why do you think it is important to keep a promise you make?

Why Do We Have Two hands?

You have to have patience to be a good teacher and a good student

Jacob wanted to show his friend Rafi what a patient man Rabbi Hillel was.

"I will give you four hundred gold coins," said Jacob to Rafi, "if you can make Rabbi Hillel lose his patience."

"Oh, I can make anybody lose their patience," answered Rafi.

So, one Friday, Rafi went over to Rabbi Hillel's house.

He was sure that if he asked impossible-to-answer questions, Rabbi Hillel would lose his patience.

Rafi knocked on the Rabbi's door.

Rabbi Hillel was taking a bath. He jumped out of the bath, dried himself off, put on a bathrobe, and answered the door.

"Hello," said the Rabbi. "How can I help you?"

"My name is Rafi. I have a question to ask you."

"I will try my best to answer your question," said the Rabbi.

"Answer me this," said Rafi, with a smile. "Why are most men taller than women?"

"So they can reach things on the very top shelf," answered Rabbi Hillel immediately.

"Oh," said Rafi, and walked away.

Rabbi Hillel went back to finish his bath. Soon there was another knock at Rabbi Hillel's door.

The Rabbi got out of the bath again, water dripping from his feet.

"Who's there?" he asked, opening the door.

"It's me, Rafi. I have one more question."

"Ask, my son," said Rabbi Hillel.

"Why do some people have blond hair, and some have dark hair?"

"Because God wants some hair to look like the sun, and some hair to look like the night sky," answered Hillel.

"Oh," said Rafi, thinking what a clever answer the Rabbi had given him.

A few minutes later, Rafi returned and knocked on the Rabbi's door once more.

Out jumped Rabbi Hillel from the bath, putting on his robe, water dripping from his feet.

"Who's there?" asked Rabbi Hillel.

"It's me, Rafi. I have one more question."

"Ask, my son," smiled the Rabbi. "I like to answer your questions."

"Why," asked Rafi, "do we have five fingers on each hand?"

"So we can count, one, two, three, four, five -- twice," said Hillel, counting his own fingers.

"Huh?" said Rafi, wondering if the answer was indeed true.

As he walked away, Rafi realized that he was losing his patience.

Rafi went to knock on the Rabbi's door yet again. But before he could touch the door, the door swung open.

"Nice to see you again!" said the Rabbi, cheerfully.

"Why do we have two hands?" asked Rafi, no longer smiling.

"So we can open the door with one hand, and shake hands with our friends with the other," answered Rabbi Hillel, shaking Rafi's. "Is there anything else you wish to ask me?" added the Rabbi.

"Just one more question," said Rafi angrily. "How is it you have so much patience for my questions?"

"My son," said the Rabbi, "a teacher must have patience for everyone. After all, questions are the way people show they want to learn, so if I am to teach, I must have patience for everyone's questions."

"My friend, Jacob, was right," said Rafi. "You are the most patient man in the world. This was a good lesson, even if it cost me four hundred gold coins."

"Four hundred gold coins?" asked the Rabbi. "How did that happen?"

"I'm glad you asked me that question," said Rafi, smiling.

THINKING THOUGHTS

* What lesson did Rafi learn from Rabbi Hillel?
* When was the last time you were patient?
* Why do some people say "There's no such thing as a silly question?" Do you agree with them?

What A Few Words Can Do

Sometimes you have to know when to say, "I don't agree!"

I don't like Aaron," Rachel announced to her friends during recess at school.

"Why?" asked Sarah, taking out her jacks.

"Because Aaron stepped on my toe, and it hurt a lot," answered Rachel.

"Yesterday, I was speaking to Aaron and he made believe he didn't hear me," Debby added, bouncing a basketball.

Daniel didn't want to be the only one not saying

anything bad about Aaron, so he said, "And he always expects someone else to clean up his mess during playtime."

"That's true," everyone agreed.

"Well, I think Aaron is very nice," said Robert.

"You think everyone is nice," Rachel scolded. "What's so nice about Aaron?"

"One day when I fell, he helped me get up and brush the dirt off my clothes," Robert told her.

"Well, that's just one time," said Rachel.

"But talking badly about Aaron," said Robert, "will only make him feel bad."

"Who's going to tell him?" Rachel asked.

"I'm sure he will find out from somebody," Robert told her.

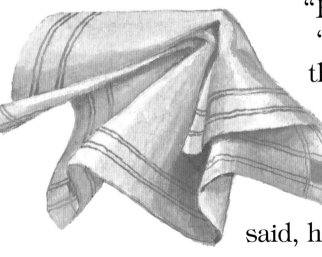

"How do you know that?"

"I'll show you. Here's something my mother taught me. Who's got a tissue?" asked Robert.

"A tissue?" echoed Rachel.

"I've got a tissue," Daniel said, handing it to Robert.

Robert tore the tissue into many little pieces. Then he said to his friends, "Pretend these are the nasty words you say about Aaron. When I throw them into the air –"

The children watched as the wind carried the pieces of tissue up into the air and far away from them.

"You think the pieces of tissue will land on the ground, but the wind blows the pieces all over the place. That's what happens when we say bad things about someone. You think your words are going only into the other person's ears.

"But before you know it, the person you tell tells another person and that person tells another person, until everyone knows what you said - even Aaron."

The children understood. They felt sad that they had said such nasty things about Aaron.

"From now on, I'll only look for good things to say about Aaron," Sarah said.

"Actually, I think Aaron helped me with my math homework a few weeks ago," Daniel revealed.

"I suppose anyone can accidentally step on your toes," Rachel declared.

Just then Aaron walked by.

"Hi, Aaron!" everyone shouted.

"Come and join us," Rachel urged.

"It sure is nice to see that you want me to join you," Aaron said, sniffling because he had a cold.

"Here's a tissue," Rachel offered.

Then Robert put his arm around Aaron's shoulder. "Of course we want you to join us," he said. "After all, you're our friend."

THINKING THOUGHTS

* Why is it better to say nice things about people, than bad things?

* Why did Daniel say something bad about Jacob when he really didn't want to?

* What are some of the good things you could say about your friends?

The King's Shiny Ring

Sometimes people give up too soon

One morning, King Alfred decided to wear his very most favorite ring. This ring was large and beautiful, and shone as brightly as the sun.

On his way to the dining room to eat breakfast, King Alfred tripped, and his ring fell onto the floor. The king's servants rushed to pick up the ring and give it to the king. But when King Alfred looked down at his ring, he saw that it had a large scratch on it.

"Oh!" said the king to his servants in surprise. "My beautiful shiny ring is no longer smooth and shiny. It has a big scratch. What shall I do?" he asked, sadly.

"I know," said one of the king's servants. "We will call all the famous artists and jewelers in the kingdom and see if one of them can fix the ring. Then the King will be happy again."

Many famous artists and jewelers came to the king's palace, and looked at the ring. But there was nothing they could do. The ring would never look the same.

King Alfred was very sad. He thought only about his ring, and how shiny and beautiful it had been, and how it would never look the same. He could not wear it anymore.

One day a jeweler named Levi, who lived in a faraway land, was passing by the palace. He heard about King Alfred's scratched ring.

"King Alfred," said Levi the Jeweler, "I think I can make your ring beautiful and shiny again."

"You can?" asked King Alfred. "What can *you* do to my ring, when all the famous artists and jewelers in my kingdom cannot make it beautiful and shiny again?"

"I can make it beautiful," said Levi the Jeweler, "because I have learned to do things others cannot do. I see things in special ways that others do not."

King Alfred jumped with joy. "If you make my ring shiny and beautiful again, I will be a very happy king."

For several days King Alfred and his servants waited for Levi the Jeweler to come out of his special workroom. They watched the door, and waited, and waited and waited.

Still Levi the Jeweler did not come out of his workroom. "Levi the Jeweler must be working very hard on your ring," said the servants to King Alfred.

After almost a week, Levi the Jeweler opened the door of his workroom, with a big smile on his face.

"I told you I could make the ring beautiful again," he said, holding up the ring. "Here it is, better than it was before."

King Alfred and his servants walked toward Levi the Jeweler and looked at the ring very closely. The ring was truly very beautiful, even more beautiful than before.

"I did not remove the scratch," explained Levi the Jeweler. "I took my knife and carved a beautiful flower on the ring. The scratch is not a scratch any more! It is the stem of the beautiful flower."

Everyone agreed that Levi the Jeweler was a very special artist, who knew how to see things that no one else could see.

With just a little change, the ring that King Alfred thought could never be beautiful ever again had become even more beautiful than before. Levi had just looked at the scratch in a different way. And Levi had also made the King even happier than he was before.

THINKING THOUGHTS

* Why did Levi succeed when all the jewelers in the land failed?
* When did you have confidence that you could do something that others thought was too difficult?
* What do you think happens when you say to yourself "I can do it"?

Three Wishes Too Many

What you wish for may not always be the best thing for you

Elijah the Prophet was magical and could appear as anyone he wanted.

One afternoon Elijah was walking through a town and noticed a house on the street that was not as nice as the others. It had a broken gate, and the paint was peeling off the front of the house.

Elijah knocked on the front door.

When the couple who lived there opened the door, they saw a kind looking, older man.

"Please come in and have some food and drink with us," they said.

Elijah sat at the table with Sarah and Jonah. They ate a small meal of dry bread and a cup of tea.

"I am a stranger, and yet you shared with me the little food you have," said Elijah to Sarah and Jonah. "I would like to grant you three wishes."

Sarah and Jonah could hardly believe their ears. At first they did not think Elijah was telling the truth, but they decided to try anyway.

"I would like a big beautiful house," said Jonah, "So I could have enough room for all my books."

Elijah played a note on his flute, and a great big palace now stood where the tiny house had been.

Sarah saw the beautiful palace and jumped for joy. Then she looked at her old, torn clothes. "I would like to dress like a wealthy lady," she said.

Again Elijah played a note on his flute, and suddenly Sarah and Jonah were dressed in the most beautiful clothes they ever saw.

"Let's make gold our third wish," they both said.

Elijah blew the flute a third time and gold coins began to rain on the dining room table. Sarah and Jonah bent down to pick up the coins that had fallen on the floor.

When they looked up, Elijah had disappeared.

A few years later, Elijah visited the couple again to see how they were doing.

When he walked toward Sarah and Jonah's palace, he

saw that the windows were covered with large shutters, and a tall, strong guard was standing at the entrance.

Elijah knocked on the door. When Sarah and Jonah opened the door they did not recognize him.

"Go away," they said. "We don't want any strangers here!"

"Chase this man away," said Jonah to the guard.

Elijah was very sad. He was sorry he had given Sarah and Jonah the three wishes. They were no longer as nice to strangers as they were when they had been poor.

Elijah took out his flute and blew a note, and all the gold in the house disappeared.

He blew a second note, and all the beautiful royal

clothes and jewels were gone.

Elijah blew a third note, and the palace turned back into the little, old, broken-down house that had been there before.

"Look what's happened to us," Sarah and Jonah said to each other.

"Because we stopped bringing guests into our house and being kind to people who visited our town, all our wishes are gone."

From that day on, Sarah and Jonah began again to invite guests to their poor, little home, and forever after felt truly rich!

THINKING THOUGHTS

* Why did Sarah and Jonah stop inviting guests to their house after they received their wishes?
* How can inviting guests to your house make you feel rich?
* Have you ever wished for something and then realized it really wasn't what you needed?

Who Will Blow The Shofar?

Saying you're sorry to someone you might have hurt is one of the signs of a good person

It was almost Rosh Hashanah, the Jewish New Year, and everyone was busy getting ready for the holiday. People were cleaning their homes, and cooking wonderful meals. But most of all, they were getting ready to pray to God to give them a wonderful New Year.

Rabbi Greenburg knew that blowing the Shofar in the synagogue helped people pray to God. Hearing the clear Shofar blasts was like a call to pour out your heart to God.

"Tekiaaaah!" the Shofar would call. "It is Rosh Hashanah time! Time to try harder to be a kind person!"

"Shevareeeeem!" the Shofar would blare. "It is Rosh Hashanah time! Time to be extra nice to everyone!"

"Teru-aaaah!" the Shofar would shout. "It is Rosh Hashanah time! Time to ask God to forgive us for the bad things we may have done!"

But who was going to blow the Shofar? It had to be someone who could make the Shofar sing!

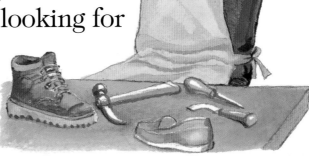

As Rabbi Greenburg was strolling through the town looking for someone to blow the Shofar, the shoemaker came out of his store. Perhaps the shoemaker will blow the Shofar for us this year, the Rabbi thought.

"Rabbi," said the shoemaker, "look at these shoes. I made the stitches so straight. It looks like a machine made it."

He is too boastful to blow the Shofar, the Rabbi realized.

Walking further, Rabbi Greenburg met the grocer. Perhaps the grocer will blow the Shofar for us this year, the Rabbi thought.

"Rabbi," said the grocer, "I get angry when people touch and smell the fruit in my store. I wish they would just buy whatever they touch."

He is too angry to blow the Shofar, the Rabbi decided.

After walking some more, Rabbi Greenburg began to worry. What will happen if I do not find anyone to blow the Shofar? But he kept on looking.

Just then, Rabbi Greenburg saw Mr. Moskowitz, the second grade teacher, talking to a group of small children. After the children left, Mr. Moskowitz turned to greet the Rabbi.

"Hello, Rabbi!" said Mr. Moskowitz.

"How are you?" asked the Rabbi.

"I am sad that I might have hurt a child's feelings. I have asked the children to forgive me if I made them feel bad this year," said Mr. Moskowitz to the Rabbi.

"Well, you are just the person I have been searching for to blow the Shofar," said Rabbi Greenburg.

"It would be an honor," Mr. Moskowitz told him.

So Mr. Moskowitz blew the Shofar in the synagogue. And everyone was very happy with the way he made the Shofar sing. Many of the people poured out their hearts to God, and looked forward to a wonderful new year.

THINKING THOUGHTS

* Why did Rabbi Greenburg think that Mr. Moskowitz was the right person to blow the Shofar?
* Why was it so important to pick just the right person to blow the Shofar?
* Describe the last time you were careful not to hurt someone's feelings.

SEVEN ANIMAL STORIES FOR CHILDREN

Stories By Theme:
Respect Modesty
Gratitude Honesty
Attitude Friendship
Responsibility

SEVEN ANIMALS WAG THEIR TALES

Stories By Theme:
Helpfulness Making Choices
Cooperation Duty
Teamwork Courage
Accepting Differences